All that is gold does not glitter,

Copyright Acknowledgements

To the following persons, we give thanks for their words that we have seen fit to quote in various sections of our book:

These Are The Clouds from The Green Helmet and Other Poems by William Butler Yeats, 1910

Sonnet 14 by William Shakespeare

Quote taken from The Dreamrealm Legacies © Jailbird

Quote taken from the English translation of Soneto XVII (Sonnet XVII) from Cien Sonetos de Amor (100 Love Poems) © Pablo Neruda ,1959

Quote taken from Other People from Fragile Things: Short Fictions and Wonders © Neil Gaiman, 2006

Quote taken from Act IV, Scene I of The Tempest by William Shakespeare

Quote by Bradley Chicho

Quote from The Lord of the Rings © J.R.R Tolkien, 1954

The character Buckbeak taken from Harry Potter © J.K Rowling, 1999

Contents

Nature
Star Light, Star Bright
Take Flight
Blue Skies, Red Clouds
The Little Things in Life

Elements
Air
Halcyon
Letting Go
When Seasons Collide

Dreams
Memento Mori
Cupping Water
The Weather Shop
Libre Enfin; Free at Last

Tidbits
Rain, Rain (Don't) Go Away
Pen and Pencil
The Dreamer's Chase
Closer To Us

Nature.

Not from the stars do I my judgment pluck,
And yet methinks I have astronomy;
But not to tell of good or evil luck,
Of plagues, of dearths, or seasons' quality;
Nor can I fortune to brief minutes tell,
Pointing to each his thunder, rain, and wind,
Or say with princes if it shall go well
By oft predict that I in heaven find.
But from thine eyes my knowledge I derive,
And, constant stars, in them I read such art
As truth and beauty shall together thrive
If from thyself to store thou wouldst convert;
Or else of thee this I prognosticate,
Thy end is truth's and beauty's doom and date.

—William Shakespeare, Sonnet 14

Star Light, Star Bright by Kailen H.

Dedication: To the boy in reindeer pyjamas under the Christmas tree. Thank you for reminding me of what Christmas can bring: not only good cheer, but also heart-warming moments with family.

May all your wishes upon the stars come true.

Star light, Star bright,
First star I see tonight,
Wish I may, wish I might
Have the wish I wish tonight.

"For my Christmas wish, I wish my sister will come home."

Happy, halcyon childhood days; haven't we all had them? Sun-kissed days and starlit nights, back when we were innocent and heartless; now but faded sepia photographs in memory's album. That was the age of insouciance; of undependable, immeasurable time that, suddenly, seemed to whoosh by on the wings of migrating swallows rather than seep through a hole in the bottom of a tin of treacle.

As children, we were always very close; closer than most siblings seven years apart were. Christmas was our favourite holiday season. The smell of freshly chopped Christmas trees in the air, their outstretched arms catching the first snowfall, hot cocoa and the traditional blackberry pie mama baked always brought smiles to our faces.

But, best loved of all, was waking up early in the morning to sit under the Christmas tree, dressed in our Christmas reindeer pyjamas, with huge smiles on our faces as we tried to decide which present to open first.

Star Light, Star Bright

"Can we put the popcorn strings on first this year?" you asked. "You promised 'cause I let you put the LED lights on, remember?"

I was rummaging through our Christmas decorations so I just nodded my head in response; I was searching for our silver star, the one we use for our version of 'christening the Christmas tree to signify a new family Christmas'.

"I can't find it!" I yelled distraught and half panicky. What if we didn't get to have the perfect Christmas because of the missing star? "Will you help me find it, Charlie? Pretty please? I don't wanna get into trouble..."

We searched high and low, right and left, under the drawers, beds and cupboards; the star was that important. It signified our family Christmas, and had been around ever since you had been born. Finally, we found it, hidden in the darkest corner of the cupboard where the decorations were kept, and covered in a thin layer of dust. Exhaling sighs of relief, we fell back against the plush cream carpet, giggling and then outright laughing.

I was happy to see you laugh so joyfully; I hadn't seen you laugh that much in a long time. I could still remember the time when I was eight, when I could clearly hear the hushed shouting behind closed doors and the tears, hearing your cries even though you tried to keep them quiet.

"Come on, small fry, let's officially 'start' Christmas shall we?" I grimaced at that nickname—I know I'm small for my age, there's no need to constantly remind me—but followed suit anyway.

Star Light, Star Bright

Together, with you standing on a chair and I standing on two, we carefully placed the age-old star on the very top of the Christmas tree.

"There," you said with a hint of pride.
"Another perfect Christmas to come."

That was our last Christmas together as a family. In the duration of the next few months, the arguments got more heated, and you cried every night. One night, the argument turned into a shouting match, and then came a loud THWACK. Silence, and a door slamming; I was certain you had gotten slapped.

When I peeped outside my room the next morning, glass was strewn on the floor, and all was silent. I crept on my tippy-toes into your room and to my horror, I found it empty. The bed was cold, and your cupboard empty. At first I thought you were simply playing hide-and-seek, so I proceeded to look for you in all our hiding spots. Mama asked me what I was doing and, when I explained it, she had tears streaming down her face. As an eight-year-old, I couldn't understand why she was crying. After all, you were only playing hide-and-seek with me. Mama knelt down on her knees, hugged me tightly and told me that it wasn't my fault.

"What isn't my fault, mama?" I don't understand.
"Amy love, Charlie has run away."

I couldn't—wouldn't believe it. How could you run away? How could you just *leave me?* I must admit to throwing a tantrum after mum told me. I'd stomped all around the house, wailing and crying, until I stepped on a piece of broken glass and cut my foot. Even then, I still couldn't believe it. It *hurt.*

Star Light, Star Bright

It was like a dark shadow came and settled on my heart. You didn't even come to say goodbye, not even a note.

You just left.

Incidentally, when I tried looking for the family Christmas star the next year, I couldn't find it. Funny, that. Christmas was never the same again for the following years. Mum never bought another star, and Christmas now seemed dreary without you around. I make a wish every Christmas, birthday and at night, on every star, in the hope that you will finally come home. It hasn't been fulfilled yet, but it will.

It's Christmas once more, and we're sitting in the living room watching The Great Christmas Movie Marathon (our new Christmas tradition since you left). We'd stay up all night watching Christmas classics like It's a Wonderful Life, Frosty the Snowman and The Night Before Christmas.

Right now, we're in the middle of watching Father Christmas. He's just attending The Annual Snowman's Party when the doorbell rings.

The door bell rings once, twice, three times (we were playing rock, paper, scissors to decide who would open the door and I lost) before I finally get up to answer it.

You still look the same as you did seven years ago, only taller and older (no insult intended). You still have the same hair, and you still give the same lopsided smile.

"Who's at the door, dear?" mum's asking. I do not give her an answer. I only hold the door open, for Charlie; my darling older sister that has finally come home.

The house is full of tears and joy this Christmas, and I honestly cannot think of a better way to celebrate. At last, our family is back together.

Is it any wonder that I finally found our Christmas star buried under wires behind our television just that night? Christmas miracle? I think not. It's the stars, it's always the stars.

Take Flight by Viper S.

Dedication: A million thanks to Elise Richards, the creator of a comic strip from where I got the inspiration to this story, and who graciously permitted me to borrow her beautiful ideas.

I love her.

Always have, always will.

My first memory of her is still fresh, like dew on leaves on the first morning of spring or the smell of the air after the rain subsides. Still fresh, like the red streaks on your arm.

They sedated me, the Evil Ones. When I woke up, groggy and dazed, I was in a whole new place. Different cage, different faces, different scents—different everything. I think it must've been the seventh time they moved me.

I never bothered to make new friends, for I'd have to leave them or they'd have to leave me in the end—or; if not now, later. I decided after my third transfer that I'd rather save the heartbreak and remain alone. In my opinion, being lonely hurts less than being left or doing the leaving.

The morning I arrived, I opened my heavy eyelids to a new world. As my vision cleared, I noticed an unfamiliar face looking keenly at me. She was a pretty brunette, with pretty sapphire eyes and raindrops on her lashes. She noticed me awaking from my slumber and moved a few inches closer to my cage. She seemed to smile at me, and *only* me. I didn't know why. Receiving any amount of attention felt weird.

After awhile, she left, and I forgot her by dinner time.

Take Flight

I was surprised when she came back the next day. She gazed at me the same way she did the day before, eyes like gems filled with curiosity and wonder. And she just stood there, gazing, watching me. She did the same thing for the next three days.

I started expecting her to come, looking forward to her visits. I remember her watchful eyes, light and kind, and her smile, her lips curving and her eyes crinkling at their corners every time I licked her finger.

She watched me for about 13 dinners, my fondness for her rising with each visit.

My take for her grew into love and loyalty the day she brought me home with her. She took me into her care, gave me happiness and become my friend; even if she was my first *and only* friend, it was more than enough for me.

I adapted to my new home quickly, and accustomed myself to my master's routines. I remember the first time I was home alone. My master had to leave the house for work. Her leaving meant me being alone for a long time. No matter, I got used to it, putting up with this sad and solemn occasion.

I'd play around in the house, turning our home into the Amazon, the ocean or my puppy kingdom. I would try listening to what our neighbours were doing but I stopped after hearing a meow one day. Eventually, after conquering rough terrains, battling imaginary zombies and saving the dog-damsel in distress, I'd take a nap, awaiting her return.

When she finally does, I hear her from the elevator; the unmistakable rhythm of her pace, the jingling of the house keys and the slight hum of her tired sighs.

Take Flight

Seeing the door swing open to permit her entrance was always one of my favourite things. I would welcome her home and, she would give me a kiss and a hug, telling me she missed me, too.

Those were the Good Days. Days when she was happy and smiling all the time. Days when she would let me share her bed, provided I didn't drool on her favourite duvet. Days that only exist in my memories now.

In the mornings, I'd fetch her the papers and she'd read them aloud as I pretended to understand. She would cook breakfast while I waited patiently for her to ration a quarter of it with me and share a bottle of milk.

She'd take a bath, and there would always be white fluffy things and circles that float in the air. I would try to catch them, never failing to pop every single time. My master would laugh every time one bursts in my face.

She would sing as she got ready, the apartment resounding with her voice. And before she left home, she would give me a kiss and a "See you later!"

But, like I said, those were the Good Days, and when there is good, bad will follow.

One day, she brought home a person. He played with me and gave me good tummy rubs. He even got me a ball and we played fetch. I liked this person very much, and as it seems, so did my master. I was beginning to realize as time went by that she loved him more than she loved me. And that thought alone was the most disturbing thought I've ever had.

Take Flight

The person moved into our house and into our lives, as fast as a tornado finishing off a little town. My master and the person spent every waking minute together; eating, cooking, playing, singing, and ignoring my existence.

Morning breakfasts were shared without me and I had to get used to sleeping on the floor. My master stopped telling me she loved me and I started to believe that she *did* stop loving me. But nevertheless, I would never stop loving her.

My master and the person started shouting a lot and throwing things at each other. I don't know what they were talking about, but they didn't look happy. My master would sit on the couch and water would trickle from her eyes and all I could do was to sit beside her and cuddle with her, hoping it made her feel better. After all, there's nothing much a dog can do.

Soon the person moved out and I thought my master would be happy again. But I was wrong. Those were when the Bad Days started.

The Bad Days were when my master never ate, never slept and never left her bed. She would just roll around among the covers and pillows and more water would flood from her eyes. She never told me why though. Maybe she did; I just couldn't understand.

My master never sang on days like this, just blasted noisy tunes from that black box of hers that hurt my ears. Days like this, she forgot to feed me, or talk to me, or kiss my head and hug me. She forgot to wake up and love me.

Take Flight

But just because she forgot about me, it didn't mean I did, or should have. One night, I saw my master do something…peculiar. She took a metal rectangle and dragged it down her arm. Red liquid trailed from behind like little red ants and I knew it was her blood. I tried to lick her lines at first, trying to ease her pain, but she would just push me away and make more lines. *Why isn't she stopping? Doesn't it hurt?* I would ask myself as she drew the red lines over and over and over again. She did it almost every night. When she ran out of space on her arms, she drew the lines on her legs instead.

This morning, she made breakfast for the first time in what feels like an eternity. She actually stayed with me while I ate, looking at me the same way she did when we first met, except now with much more solemn eyes. She let me drink a whole bottle of milk and didn't tell me off for dripping it all over the floor. She played with me the whole afternoon and kept giving me treats. She even let me lick her lines. She started smiling and giggling a little everytime I tried standing on my hind legs and end up falling over. I realized it was the first time in ages since I heard her laugh. *Master is finally getting better!*

But now, I'm getting a little worried. Awhile ago, when the sun was still up, my master told me she loved me and then went into her room. I thought nothing of it, thought that she was going to take a nap, so I continued chewing on my bone. When the sun disappeared and my master still hadn't came out from her room, I waited in front of her door. Waited, waiting, until now.

I don't think I can take it anymore, so I decide to open the door with the trick I learned some time ago. I stand up, put my front paws on the door handle and give it a downward push. The doors swing open, and if I were human, I would gasp.

Master is flying! She looks so beautiful, her hair, falling perfectly around her shoulders, and her dress billowing out around her. With the light from the lamp illuminating her from behind, my master looks like an angel. My collar is around her neck like a necklace, together with my leash tied to the ceiling fan. Maybe that's how she keeps herself from falling.
Her eyes are closed as though she is sleeping, and she has a slight smile on her face. *I get to see Master smile again. She's finally happy!*

"Hi Master! You've been trying to fly again, haven't you? It didn't work the last time, but I think you got it this time. I believe in you, master. I knew you'd be able to do it, one day," I told my master.

She doesn't respond, or even look at me.

"It's okay, Master. Enjoy yourself up there, alright?" I tell her. I start to yawn. It's getting pretty late.

"I think I'll take a nap until you come down. Goodnight, Master. I love you."

Blue Skies, Red Clouds by Kristal L.

Dedication: For the saga trees in and around St John's Hill, Melaka, that provided the inspiration and setting of this piece. May you continue to disperse your beautiful red offerings for a long time to come, that little children such as I once was, will too have memories of you and your heart-shaped, heart's-blood seeds.

I've always associated clouds with the blood-red "love seeds" of the saga tree. When we were still young enough to be obnoxious yet ignorant brats, my brother and I used to play with these saga seeds. I can still see how the glorious redness of them, picked up from the ground, spilled from our sweaty fists onto the glass-topped coffee table, which stood directly under a skylight. Tired of our games of tag and hide-and-seek, we'd lie, side by side, with our heads under the table. Light filtered down, the bright azure sky as seen through the glass in the ceiling clashing beautifully with the sun-shadowed seeds that appeared to float in the sky above, tiny almost-black drops of blood suspended in mid-air.

They're beautiful, these seeds. Or are they beads, as some say? I personally prefer to call them what they are, the tiny offspring of a stately tree, waiting for the right time to take root. Waiting for the right time to blossom, to grow higher and higher to touch the sky. They are as unhurried and unconcerned as the fluffy white clouds that pass leisurely by above. Yes, saga seeds will always be akin to clouds in my mind.

We used to pelt these seeds at one another too, my brother and I. It was our ammunition, as we fought our pretend-battles amongst the saga trees on the hill behind our house. They didn't really hurt, not even when flung hard. More... like being tickled, I'd say. The slight sting at impact wore off quickly, leaving a sort of tingling sensation. Altogether, it wasn't unlike being caressed by an icy-cold cloud, a feeling I have held dear in my memory throughout these trying months.

Boys being boys, both of us signed up as soon as we heard the rumours of approaching bloodshed. We were at the height of our youth, him having just turned eighteen and I being twenty-one. Our country, this land that we had been born into, was at stake, and we were proud to defend it at any cost. Or so we thought.

It is a terrible thing, war. You see it approaching before you hear it, the hate-filled glare of a dark cumulonimbus on an otherwise clear horizon. The glint of light off metal is like lightning; the stomp of boots marching ever onward is like thunder. They seem to be so far, yet so near. Then the storm is upon you, and blood rains down on your head like rain.

By the third day of slaughter at the front, he had gone half mad with the killing. He was little more than a child, forced to witness the horror of our comrades being struck down beside us. It was too late to pull out, too late to turn back—*too late*. By the time I'd realised he was no longer at my side, it was too late; *he* was *gone*.

He was lucky, I suppose—it was quick for him. He seemed to know it was the end, judging by the crazy smile still on his face. But there was something in his eyes, something... I don't quite know how to put it. Following his line of sight, I saw the serene sky of our childhood, the insouciant white clouds and the magnificent blue arch so very much higher above it all. And, looking down at his blood-spattered uniform, I knew exactly why he'd smiled.

Blue Skies, Red Clouds

While others saw red rain falling from the sky, as they spent their final moments here in this world, my brother saw red saga seed clouds.

It's noon, and it's swelteringly hot. Most folk sit at home, battling the heat with palm-leaf fans. But not these brothers; these soldiers, these pirates, this hero-and-sidekick duo. This is their secret time away from reality, when everything is still and silent and they are the only people in the world.

The younger one is dodging and ducking, weaving through the trees as he flees downhill. The elder, armed with a handful of saga seeds that he constantly replenishes from the abundance of them on the ground, is in hot pursuit. Their laughs and shouts are punctuated with the occasional squeal from the younger brother when a well-aimed seed hits a particularly ticklish spot. At the foot of the hill, he collapses in a heap of laughter, a few metres away from the first trees dotting the side of the hill. The elder shouts triumphantly. He continues his merciless onslaught for a while, then abruptly ceases as he skids to a halt beside his brother.

The younger one uncurls from his protective foetal position, flopping face-up in the sweet grass. He squints slightly at the bright sunlight, still chuckling weakly. The elder, who, it appears, did not spend all his seeds in the chase, suddenly lets loose a torrent of red over his brother's face. The younger gasps, choking on both his laughter and a few stray seeds that have made their way into his mouth. They are both laughing uncontrollably again by the time the elder has helped the younger into a sitting position and has whacked him on the back just a little too hard to be helpful in expelling the seeds.

"I think I swallowed one," gasps the younger brother. "Are these things poisonous or something?"

Blue Skies, Red Clouds

"Only one way to find out," grins the elder. "If you turn grey and start smelling funny tomorrow morning, we'll know." He dodges an indignant swipe, unable to control the amusement sweeping across his features.

The younger shakes his head in mock disapproval, his laughter dying away. Changing the subject, he muses, "I thought the clouds were falling from the sky, when you did that." He mimes sprinkling something.

The elder understands perfectly. "You must be spending too much time under the table, then." Cheekily, he tosses a seed at his brother, which ricochets off his face. "There! Cloud bit your nose!"

The younger shakes his head again. "You should have seen your face. It was so... so..." He searches for the word, his six-year-old vocabulary drawing up a blank. "Never mind."

His brother shrugs, impatient; nearly ten and too grown up to care. "Want to build a fort?"

"Yes!" The younger's eyes light up, the seeds forgotten.

"Race you to the top, then!" The elder takes off to cries of protest at the injustice of his head start from the younger.

They disappear amongst the trees together, racing off into a land where the world is a playground and saga seeds are clouds.

The Little Things in Life by Irene T.

Dedication: To my parents; thank you for your everlasting support in all that I do. I will cherish it always.

She remembered a time when her days revolved around the sun.

There was a time when she spent almost every morning frolicking in the field, teasing flower petals from their stems even as ankle-high blades of grass tried in vain to smack her for her naughtiness. She did not mind the way the grass whipped about her; their pushing and pulling felt vaguely like the playful waves she dipped into just once, when she was younger. The sea was close, just a ten-minute drive away from her home, but the field was closer. And so much of her activities took place in the field, out in the glorious sun.

The sun of her childhood days was nowhere near as unforgiving as the sun of her young adult years. Gone were the times when she could stay in the sun all day without getting sunburnt; nowadays it was so strong that she could feel it through the glass that imprisoned her indoors, in her hostel far away from home. Still, the sun was a constant reminder of her family, so as much as she disliked the way it baked her skin a crisp brown, she loved it just the same.

Each time the sun beat down on her she remembered the days when her mother used to play with her, either in their garden or in the field next door. Age granted her the permission to venture into the field alone (though she believed that it was merely an excuse for her mother to dote on her then-infant brother) and she used it to the fullest extent. She raced the wind; she upturned stones; she dug for 'treasure'; she napped on the bare grass and let the sun lull her to sleep. School holidays often found her in the field from dawn to dusk, at first to enjoy herself in, and later, as she grew older, to study.

School gobbled up much of her time. Even then, she refused to give up the joy that is the sun. She joined co-curricular activities that took her outdoors as much as possible. Running, jumping, ball games, javelin…she tried them all, if only to find an excuse to stay outside just a while longer. She remembered, with a quiet chuckle, how she ended up missing more classes than she attended all year long by the time she was in Form Five. Some teachers became *so* exasperated with her, but were unable to do anything about it because she was absent with valid reasons. That was the sweetest victory of her school days. Of course there were a few who brooked no excuses, and those irked her as much as she irked them; not that it mattered now, water under the bridge and all that. She still visits those teachers sometimes, whenever she returns to her alma mater during semester breaks.

Many things changed once she left secondary school. She was young, she felt free; she was excited, and yet afraid. She received a graduation gift of sorts from her parents, a sleek silver laptop, which they said would be necessary for her future tertiary education. Armed with her new gadget, she went to the field to escape her brother's rock music, and spent sunny days completing career quizzes and looking up possible courses.

Her mother's garden stayed pretty much the same throughout her formative years: bright, lively and steady in the face of time. The tiny space in front of their home splashed colours on their white-washed walls, so many colours that oftentimes the garden became the highlight of the house, instead of the building itself. Her family didn't mind, her least of all – although she was sorry to say that she did not inherit her mother's green thumb. Neither did her brother, who preferred to hole up in his room screaming and banging and booming away as if the world was about to end.

Telling a teenage boy to tone down and grow up was worse than telling a wall that it was in the way, so she did the next best thing and stayed out of the house. She never needed to tell her parents where she'd be going anymore, partially because they said she was an adult now and should make her own decisions, and also because they knew where she'd go anyway. During these times, she was introverted, preferring quality over quantity, so she spent much of her time alone, quite paradoxically outdoors. She had her brother to thank for that – not that she was sorry about it.

There were times of gloomy rain, of course, times when the sun got smothered by dark, angry clouds. Malaysia had to brave two monsoon seasons each year, and the area she lived in was buffeted by both, in varying degrees. Those days she spent indoors. When she was a child her puerile mind could not comprehend how the powerful sun could allow itself to be herded away like a silly sheep, and she raged and stomped her feet at her mother like...well, like an idiot, she supposed, but how was she supposed to know that back then?

When her own internal storm had subsided into sulks and tears, she would sit by the window and wait for the sun to peek out from behind the clouds. The sun always wins the war against its nemeses the clouds and rain; it always shines again, like a beacon in the sky. It never loses its strength, not until it is drugged asleep by the moon, and she resolved to be like it, smiling through trials and tribulations. It was by no means an easy thing to do. There were days when she felt like giving up, days when the smile she tried to tug onto her face leered at her in the mirror, but she would remember the majestic sun outside, and become stronger.

Sometimes it felt as though she smiled just to make others smile. To most, she was almost constantly cheerful, bubbly to a fault. She was a good speaker when she put her mind to it. She was an even better listener (or so they tell her; she has yet to know why or how). People who didn't know her well assumed that everything was all right in her life.

A small smile tugged at her lips as she admired the flowers in her garden.

The woman opened her eyes to a sea of white.

The sharp smell of disinfectant and the hushed sounds of people murmuring and trolleys groaning were not new to her. White, white, white. The ceiling was white, the walls were white, her bed was white; the only other *correct* colour around here – the colour that proved you belonged in here, at least for a while longer than a touch-and-go situation – was green. The hospital was splashed with green on the curtains and clothes for patients. They used to be a brighter green…lime green, she supposed, if the newer curtains were anything to go by. Now they are more grey than green, making everything and everyone clad in it look drab.

It wasn't the most inviting sight to wake up to, but beggars couldn't be choosers. The luxury of choice had escaped her for a while now, flitting just beyond her fingers like a naughty fairy. She was beginning to doubt that she would ever catch it. This resigned acceptance she kept to herself, hidden behind a serene mask. She would not, *should not* make anyone sadder than they already were, not if she could help it.

Her gaze drifted to the table at her bedside, and she blinked. Once, twice. Then, slowly, she reached out for the foreign object, determined to ignore the way her almost-fleshless hand shook worse than a leaf in the wind. Foreign *objects*, she corrected herself, as she spied a note on the table. She picked it up to read.

Dear mother, it said, in a familiar, nostalgic scrawl, *I dropped by to visit in the morning, but you were sleeping and I didn't want to disturb you. Shawn sends you his love.*

I'll come back later in the evening. The book I pre-ordered for you will be arriving today; I'll pick it up before I come, so you'll have some new reading material to last you a while...though knowing you, you'll probably finish it by tomorrow anyway.

I'm no good at gardening – here the woman shook her head, because her daughter was okay at gardening, really, if not brilliant at it – *and the garden is looking rather forlorn already. Less flowers bloomed. I tried my best...I just don't know where I've gone wrong! (I know you're thinking that it can't possibly be that bad because I'm 'acceptable' by your standards – and just so you know, I still disagree!)*

You've probably seen it already, but I've set a little surprise for you beside this note. It's the first one to bloom. I'll take it as a good omen. Hopefully it'll last you a few days.

Like mother, like daughter, yes? You taught me to love the sun, all those years ago, so I know you love it too. For now on, I will bring the sun to you, to cheer you up.

The Little Things in Life

The real sun's still waiting for us out there. We'll enjoy it together someday for sure.

Until later then.

Mia.

The woman fingered the petals of the sunflower and smiled through fresh tears.

Elements.

Fire stands for power and determination and loneliness.

Air stands for freedom and longing and wishing.

Earth stands for strength and peace and silence.

Water stands for deception and temptation and change.

–Monroe Fletcher

Air by Viper S.

Dedication: This piece is inspired by and also dedicated to someone precious who gives meaning to words like "missing you until it hurts" or "I hate you...but I love you". The someone who gives me something to look forward to each day I wake up and the someone who also makes me realize that overthinking is dangerous; emotionally, mentally, and physically.

"It's not like I'm gone. I am still with you, in your heart." "Think of me, and I will think of you. Think of us, our memories. And I will be back before you know it." "Though you can't see me, I am still with you. Always with you," You tell me every week, or something along those lines. Some weeks, I hear them almost every day. You keep it interesting for me though; changing words to give me peace. At least you don't bore me with the same speech over and over again. As I lie in bed, *Florence and The Machine* plays from my radio. *I've been a fool and I've been blind..* They tell me I'm oblivious. "Don't you see? He'll pick you up just to knock you down again." "All he wants is to show you off to his friends." I refuse to believe them. Like I usually do, I start to overthink, and like the way it usually ends, it never ends well.

I am thinking that when you are always with me, you aren't; physically yes, but your mind is not really *here*. You always were hot or cold, sometimes even in between. One minute, you'd be happy, charming. Our conversations would be filled with humour, and we'd laugh like we had never laughed before. The next minute, you'd be cold. You would look at me as if my very existence annoys you. You change as fast as one breathes, seeming like you inhale emotions from the air. You inhale the wrong air and it fills you, surges through you, and it becomes you. Like air, you never see it, you just know it is there. Around us, with us, next to us, whatever. But what is the

Air

point of just knowing, assuming, that air is in fact there? I wonder if anyone longs to see air, to actually hold it, embrace it. Not in the form of molecular drawings, or compressed in a balloon, or in the form of bubbles trying to resurface from the water, but air itself. That's how I see you, like air. Air cannot be seen, but it is here. When the air is cold, I cringe and shiver, longing for heat. But when the air is hot, it makes me angry, frustrated. Pissy. It makes me lash out at everyone around me, or at myself. When the air is lukewarm, naturally I don't feel a thing. And it doesn't bother me, to not be able to *feel*. Only when I'm lucky, will the air be warm and cosy. But it only lasts for a day or two. You cannot touch air, and I yearn for touch. Your touch.

I go through eventless days, silent meals and lonely nights. On days that don't seem so bad, I take walks. But when I pass couples in the park, lying together on the green pastures, limbs intertwined, I always find myself regretting leaving the confines of my home. I drop my gaze to the dull grey of the pavement, unable to look happiness in the eye. A clichéd arrow through the heart- the pain of knowing that our paths rarely ever often diverge from the grey, never ventured into precious emeralds and gold, treasures you get from daring to take that step off the sidewalk. We played it safe, and now I can't even fathom what lies beyond this grey world you leave me in. I let myself ponder upon the what if's, the how's and the why's. *Why is he always gone? Why does he act that way? How sure am I that he will come back? And what if he doesn't? What if he's gone for good? What am I going to do without him? Why do I need him so much?*

Flashbacks. I hate them. I remember when we first met, we were our exact opposites. He was quiet and shy and I was always socializing at full throttle. We hated each other. I would

Air

throw insults at him at every opportunity I had, and he would just brush them off. I would make snide comments about everything he did, said, ate, drank. Everything. But as the attacks multiplied, my liking towards him did too. And we became friends. And even more after that. I had no idea how it happened. It was so quick. Another flashback; rooftop, blue skies, windy day. It was just me and him, best friends just hanging out. The rooftop was our usual chill spot where we'd talk about everything and anything. We hung our legs over the edge and just talked. "Don't sit too far off the edge, alright? Wouldn't want you falling off," he said to me, smiling. I laughed. "I would've thought you'd be delighted to be rid of me." He suddenly came really close, too close. I held my breath and waited for his reply, but he just kept silent. And then he..

I push the memory to the far back of my mind. I don't miss anything else but your lips at this very moment. Who knew that soft-spoken boy would be the man I am missing tonight. I think I have always been too much for him. Too overwhelming, too outspoken, too loud, too passionate, too honest, too this, too that. He is the warm, gentle breeze of Fall, and I am the untamed wild waters of the Pacific that splash over cliffs and pull in what I want or need. And I feel that right now that is all we are...elements coexisting.

I look out the window and see the soft, pale sky crying inky blue tears. The silhouettes of every nook and cranny around me whispered and beckoned. There was a humming in my heart and a yearning in my head, and the wind carries memories I wanted to snatch from myself. It is nights like this when I cry myself to sleep. Accumulated days of nothingness, longing and yearning for.. for what? His presence? His touch? Wanting him back here in my arms, in my bed?

Air

And what would I get if he's here with me? Brief joy? Or his usual tantrums? You are unpredictable, yes, yet, very…you are 'here', but cannot be seen. Like air, you can ignite fires, create shivers, bring warmth and unbearable heat. You have the ability to wreak havoc.

And just like air is to everyone else, like you are to me; I need you, and I cannot live without you.

Halcyon by Irene T.

People often mistake her for her mother. It's not so bad when the reference is in writing, because then her name will be spelled with a small 'E', as in earth, as opposed to her mother's Earth, complete with a capitalised 'E'. It is when the reference is made verbatim that people get confused.

That's okay most times, she thinks, because Earth *is* her mother; she is a part of Earth as much as the rest of her siblings. Her brother, the water, is closest to her. They have never been separated since the day they were born. Together they form the surface of Earth, with her crusting over her mother's mantle and her brother curling, as unobtrusively as possible, in her numerous nooks and crannies. She is ugly, she knows, with all the mountains and valleys and plains that pockmark her body, and she doesn't care about it because she was born that way. Her brother tries to help her regardless, blanketing as many dips as he can with his smooth, fluid body. Dolines, lakes, ponds...they are proof of his love for her, just as how his rivers become the tears she cannot cry.

She, in turn, is the container for her brother. Without her, her brother will probably go mad, aimless and shapeless in the absence of a physical container. As it is, he is never fully with her; some part of him is always in the air, or in the clouds that police the amount of water on her. Rainy moments are when her brother is most lucid. That is when he regales her with tales of far-fetched places deep within her. She is a large entity, befitting her status as the older sibling; her dominance in size is offset by the fact that her brother is free to travel as he pleases, so long as she provides him guidance. She is sentient but immobile, while her brother is dreamy and free to travel wherever he pleases.

Halcyon

It has been keyed into her, this ability to guide her gullible, flexible brother even though she has not seen many of the places he tells her about. Some might call it instinctive. She doesn't care what people think; as long as both of them are happy, she is content. Or at least she *was* content, before the creatures that call themselves 'men' started to spread across her body like a rash. They are large in number, although this is eclipsed by their ignorance of the well-being of nature. They cut deep into her body to steal her precious stones; they blast her sides with dynamite to get sand and coal and later, natural gas; then they throw whatever by-products they do not want into her brother, the water. The two of them suffer Man in silence.

Most of the time, at least. Sometimes when they feel like having a temper tantrum, they wrought some natural disasters—with their mother's permission, of course—just to remind the humans just where they stand: nature is their host, and they, Man, are merely tenants who rent the space they live in. Alone, one man makes barely a dent in nature, but when they heave their cumulative, destructive power against her and her brother—ah , that is when they suffer. So she isn't particularly sorry when she shakes her body a little to claim humans whole, or when they get thrown into her brother's seas to drown under his blanket of waves. It sounds cruel, but she consoles herself, often effectively, that their actions are essentially reactions to the havoc wrought by man. They have done no wrong—these were acts of self-preservation.

Even with both of them throwing their weight around, humans are like the cockroaches they detest so much; to nature they are like insufferable insects that just *refuse* to die! They claim to grow smarter with every discovery they make...but to her, their idea of 'growing smarter' involves too much devastation to actually yield good enough results.

Every time she gets riled up by such thoughts, her brother will lap at the edges of her body, hoping to placate her. She acquiesces, most times, if only because she knows her mother will not be happy if she wiped out too much of the Earth's population all at once. Maintenance of equilibrium and all that. She finds it tedious.

She watches their evolution warily, wearily. Warily, because despite her size she can still be harmed, and they've been doing a great job so far; wearily, because she has never experienced such extensive damage in so short a time, not in the thousands of years when molluscs and dinosaurs crawled across her huge surface (that is, if you discount the crashing of the meteor that started the Ice Age). Very little of what Man has achieved actually preserves nature. They seem more bent on being 'sucking vampires', and she hates them for that. Humans are ungrateful brats, she concluded with a sniff.

She has no eyes to see how humans are wrecking her body, but she can *feel*. Usually she tries to push those feelings into a corner of her mind, because there is one constant message that she does not wish to receive: pain. She hurts all over. Humans are worse than her mother's scalding lava, which she used to receive quite often for recalcitrance. What's worse, they are actually slowly learning how to detect and avoid those natural disasters. She sulked for a long time when she realised that.

Their forays into her depths have grown even more extreme. She feels the rumbling of huge machines building other huge machines; she feels the millions of steps the humans take as they scurry about like so many ants in concrete prisons –

factories, they call them—to complete manufacturing processes. She also feels many things foreign to her. One day, during one of his lucid moments, her brother tells her all about Man's new inventions: cars that trundle along sandy, stony or tarred roads; new trinkets that last a long time and glint in the sun - she huffs indignantly at that, because it is *her* tin and *her* bauxite they are using to make those things, or at least they *were* hers before they stole them from her—and also the making of warfare.

Her brother also speaks of the Industrial Revolution that is roaring forward in full force. She knows, somewhere deep inside, that she should accept the beings that depend on her for life, something her mother often preached back when she was much, much younger. But she cannot. She cannot, because every time an iota of acceptance (not forgiveness, never forgiveness, she thinks) traitorously sneaks into her mind, man comes up with a new way to torture her, to kill her in their naked greed for fortunes that are ultimately even more fleeting than the lives of humans themselves.

The irony of it all is that she cannot really die. Sure, man can poison her, bomb her, mutilate her, but in the end she will not die. She will persevere, long after this generation and his children and his grandchildren have expired. It is in her nature to survive. (Even if it hurts.)

Her brother is facing the same fate as she is, in different yet similar ways. Still he continues to spin stories of the people who dot her surface. She doesn't know why, but her brother does not despise humans as she does. It is his dreamy nature, perhaps, that allows him to be as complacent as he is now. Certainly he seems happier than she is, in that lackadaisical way of his. Humans are facing trying times, he tells her, as he bubbles out of a brook for fun. They are at war. Wars, in plural, even.

She sniffs and tells him he does not care. After all, it was she who has to bear the brunt of their petty skirmishes. She drinks their vile-tasting blood and reclaims the weapons that were made out of *her* resources, disgusted but pleased. Men are killing themselves without her intervention like the bloodthirsty creatures that they are.

And yet, after all the wars are over and peace finally falls upon them, and by extension, upon her, she finds herself changing her opinion of them. Out of the blue, people start noticing her. They notice how much they are harming her with her ignorance. She quaffs the attention eagerly, waiting to see what will change.

It is by no means a fast process. They have ravaged her for so long that they find it difficult to change their ways now. But it is better than nothing. They probe her with various gadgets; they stick monitors all over her to check out her condition; more importantly, they raise awareness amongst themselves, so that the next generation will, hopefully, avoid repeating the mistakes of their forefathers.

Even now they haven't completely stopped taking too much from her. She burbles her disagreement, but otherwise stays her hand because it is still better than how they had treated her a few centuries prior, during their supposedly life-changing Industrial Revolution. It is too much, too much. They are taking way more than she can replenish, and now they—yes , *they*, not she—are feeling the backlash. Their movements to curb their greedy behaviour are becoming more harried, their efforts to become frugal are becoming more intense...but whether that is enough, she does not know yet.

She lets them try to restore her regardless. After all, she cannot die, so what is the worst that they can inflict on her now that they are not destroying her as badly as before?

In the end, she will prevail where humans cannot. She cannot die, regardless of how humans are dramatising her impending death. Right now they are partially blinded, focusing more on the other forms of life on her, rather than on her ailing body. They seem to have forgotten that she is the reason they exist at all. But that's okay.

She doesn't die; she merely takes on a new form, that's all

Letting Go by Kailen H.

Dedication: For the souls still holding on to that one person that might not be good for you. Happiness is a state of mind, a golden state of mind. You deserve to be happy. But, you must let go and let the moving waters carry you to your new chapter in life.

Anchorage (noun): The desire to hold on to something as it passes, like trying to keep a grip on a branch in the middle of a rushing river. Feeling the weight of the current press against your chest while your peers float downriver shouting over the gush or rapids: "Let go—you'll be okay—just let go."

I love coming down to the beach just to walk along the shore and watch the waves sweep the sand, leaving only white tendrils of foam as it returns to the sea. I've always thought of the ocean as calming; even with its ever-changing currents and tides, I think it's very peaceful. Today, I sit on the beach where sand meets sea. The splashing of water against rock settles into a steady rhythm—splash, swossh, splash, swossh…soothing my chaotic thoughts.

A child's laughter rings out in the distance, sounding eerie in the silence; a single sound of joy on an almost empty beach.

There, at the edge of the ocean, not even three feet away from me, the letters "K loves D" are drawn onto the wet sand, and it's as if the water cannot touch it; cannot erase it from the realm of the living. It is the sight of those words that draws me back to memories of my past.

"Time is fluid here."
-From Fragile Things by Neil Gaiman

Letting Go

Days blew by like the softest wind, and frustration scuttled into the crook of the corners of my crooked heart. There was so much I wanted to say, but had no words to say it. I gave so much... even though I knew I would receive little in return. Whenever I talked to you, my heart told my head, *"Let love grow,"* but my head told my heart *"This time, no. This time, you have to **let go**"*. Like a devil-and-angel conscience on my shoulder, they bickered. Oh how they bickered.

But how do I let go? Has there ever been a reason for this insistent longing in one's chest? There were times when I thought I could feel my soul pressing against my skin, filling my insides with wonder and colours so vivid, more vivid that I could imagine.

And there were times where I wondered if the happiness I felt inside my soul would trickle out of my skin because I wasn't sure that my body could hold so much happiness. And if it were to break free, would it turn out to be a single euphonic sound? Would it be as luminous as shards of our shining moon, or as gentle as the soft voice of a bird ensnared to its cage for all of its days?

You made me feel so small yet gigantic, just beginning yet endless, empty and full and oh so human. You were there when things got rough and you gave me a hand even though I didn't want it. But more than that, you made me feel what I wanted to feel; loved and alive.

"I love you as certain dark things are supposed to be loved. In secret, between the shadow and the soul".
-Pablo Neruda

Some nights, when I looked out my window at night to watch the moon and stars, was it any surprise that I thought about

Letting Go

you? Your smile haunts my dreams even when I'm awake, your humour and the way you laugh. The way you instantly made me feel better after a long day. We had only been on 'dates' (out to eat and/or a movie) a couple of times but I couldn't let you go. It was as if I *needed* you.

The emotions I felt existed in small ripples over the black surface, igniting feelings of melancholy and conflictions, dripping with doleful undertones of peace. And I would decide to let you go, but then regret it and snatch you back because I didn't want you to leave. That continued until I became fed up and one day, I just locked you—or rather the memory of you—in a treasure chest at the back of my mind. I thought that maybe, just maybe, I could keep you but not think of you that way. I realize now that by doing that, I'd only thought of you more vividly when something reminded me of you.

You were my first love, the only boy I had exchanged "I love you" with. I didn't realize back then that "I love you" meant "I love you as a friend". Maybe I've watched too many movies and read too many books. And maybe I expected a fairytale ending all too soon.

My misconception blind-sided me enough that I didn't see the hole I was digging for myself. By the time I did see it, I was already in too deep with no way out. I suppose I was being foolish then for ignoring all the warnings.

Everyone around could see what was going on except me. They told me, "He is no one. You can do so much better."
"He's not good enough. I don't approve."

"Don't get attached, you'll just end up sad."

But it's not the attachment that hurts, is it? It's the *detachment*. Detachment; funny, the first thing that came to mind was abandonment and loneliness. I never understood what they meant when they said, "Don't get attached". How can one *not* get attached to a person, or object?

You are very much attached to something when you're holding it, or engulfed in it. Like a hand in the water, it is submerged in water—surrounded by it, even. Some say that water leaves no impression on the hand when it is lifted out of the water because it is not attached to hand.

I disagree.

When the hand is in the water, surrounded by it, it seems to me that it is *very* attached to the hand. Yes; water leaves very little of itself on said hand, just like we leave a little of ourselves on people and things we touch. But, I found that the hand and water part 'clean', because as soon as one *wants* to leave, there can be no holding on, as there can be no attachment other than the mutual action of being together.

Then I tried to not think about you, talk to you, miss you. But—I—I did. Miss you, I mean. I missed you a lot. And it turned out horribly wrong, because, during that whole time, I refused to let you go, but forced myself to try to forget everything you meant to me. When the sun set and thoughts filled my mind, I sat alone in my room, as the nights passed by as slow as a caterpillar inching its way on a thousand-mile stretch; completely miserable.

I buried my grief in the floorboards of my soul while everyone was sleeping, only to have it slither up again and eat away at my insides. I didn't know what I was doing wrong, but

Letting Go

I knew it was something because I was destroying myself from the inside out.

I'm not quite sure when I pulled myself out of that stupor, and I'm not quite sure how; however, I know now that a 'clean' parting doesn't mean forcing the other into a decision to leave, but both coming to terms with each other; accepting. My head needed to come to terms with my heart before either could leave the other alone; they needed to accept that they both had the same goal, and they need to work together. And they did. I realized in my own time that I'm happy just being a friend—happy and proud.

We don't talk much now, but it doesn't bother me like it did before, because I found that I make a much better friend than I do as someone who loves romantically. But it doesn't stop me from loving you just as much.

And so I say goodbye, let go and embrace new moments. Just as the waves of the ocean that kiss the shoreline fade back into its salty depths, wiping away the words drawn into the sand by children, I say *"I'm not afraid to let go* now." And, when I do, it feels as if a great weight has been lifted from my shoulders, and I can finally enjoy the ride downstream that doesn't stop.

I feel *alive*.

My parting words to the rock, my anchor that kept me down: *"Goodbye to those memories, goodbye to the past; hello change and hello tomorrow."*

The sun's rays streak across the sky in a myriad of oranges, pinks and purples as it gracefully sets. By now, the waves have washed the drawn out letters leaving only a shoreline wiped

Letting Go

clean. And, right there, the tide curls around my body, washing away the past and leaving only today and the future for me to look forward to. In the midst of the waves splashing lightly against the shore and the quiet echo of the open sea, I feel as if I've finally come home.

When Seasons Collide by Kristal L.

Dedication: This piece is dedicated to one who is both a good friend and a good rival, in hope that it will serve to enlighten him on the wisest, most beneficial means of dealing with his Summer.

May he be less of a weasel and more of a fox when dealing with his eagle.

He found her on the steps behind the house, her face in her hands.

Hidden in plain sight, I see.

Oblivious to the startled jerk of her shoulders at his sudden telepathic connection, he continued, *Right under our noses, too. You, my dear, have clearly mastered the art of invisibility.* He reached over to clap her on the back.

Abruptly, Summer shied away. *Don't touch me!* Her flickering orange-red edges flared slightly in alarm. *You're ice, you utter idiot! I'd melt you!*

Shrugging, Winter's white, densely packed form shifted to a clear liquid one, then solidified once more into the tiny cold crystals. *Actually, I'm water. Ice is but a branch of my prime element.* The last he said proudly, as if being of water was a huge accomplishment.

Then, if you touch me, you'll put me out. Summer blinked warily.

Not if you make me evaporate first.

When Seasons Collide

Well, if you don't want to go up in smoke, all you have to do is not touch me.

He sighed. *Do you always have to be right?*

If you put it that way, yes.

A pause. Silence.

Has Spring left yet?

Winter nodded. *Autumn passed by, and you know how Spring is. Those two lovebirds—or, rather, that one infatuated earth elemental. She'll never catch Autumn, however long and hard she tries.*

I should've gotten a lift from him just to make Spring mad. She smiled wryly. *Then again, perhaps it's better that I didn't. He'd have wanted to know what happened.*

And Autumn can't keep a secret, sighed Winter. *That pesky wind elemental. I don't know how you stand him.*

Summer laughed; a harsh, bitter sound. *He's the only one I can touch without destroying, or being destroyed myself. Even then, there's always the risk of him putting me out entirely or me completely burning him up. Not much wonder he's my only ally, is there?*

Winter glanced sideways, lowering himself onto the step. *What actually happened between you and Spring? I got the impression that she set you off, but the details... elude me.*

When Seasons Collide

Summer's eyes blazed a furious white; fire at its most dangerous. *She nearly destroyed an entire city and a neighbouring town with one of her careless landslides, that's what. And she was just so infuriatingly cool about the whole affair that I sent a couple of trees up in smoke. She even had the nerve to tell me to calm down. Honestly! I almost lost it.*

She paused, obviously still struggling to control her flames. Beside her, Winter edged away slightly, cautious of the rising temperature. *Which is when you very conveniently barged in the door so I could slip out here and finish off the rest of the forest in peace.* Her eyes had turned fierce, hard; a smouldering pile of dynamite ready to explode at the slightest hint of cynicism from Winter.

But he merely nodded in acknowledgement of her actions. No comments, no criticism, no snide remarks; how very unlike the snarky, silver-tongued Winter she knew. *I personally prefer slowly freezing small animals to death, or drowning them—slowly—when I get... put off, you might say. But to each his (or her, in your case) own, I suppose.*

Summer shrugged. *We're opposing elements.*

He was silent for a moment, choosing his words with great care. *They say opposites attract, you know.*

When she made no reply, nor any inclination that she had heard, he went on boldly. *I envy Autumn, really. As you said before, he's the only one who can touch you without... dire consequences... for one party or the other.*

Summer sighed softly. *Perhaps.* Their eyes locked, unspoken words passing between them. Then, as if on cue, they reached out to each other.

Their fingertips hovered, faltered; a hair's breadth between them

We can't, she whispered. *Not without destroying ourselves and all that we hold dear.*

Winter nodded, swallowing thickly. *And...?*

We go on, longing for what we cannot have, as all the seasons must. Summer wore a look of resigned sorrow.

Winter glanced at everything and nothing in particular, eyes unfocused. Somewhere, an unseasonal thaw burst a river's banks, drowning a family of water rats—slowly.

Summer watched him. *Winter. Snap out of it.*

He sighed, the sudden deluge of icy water slowing. Just in time, too; Autumn suddenly appeared before them, skidding to a halt in the backyard.

Summer, where the heck were you?! You're twelve days overdue in twenty-six countries! They're all blaming it on global warming now. Autumn's words came out in a rush; he had to repeat himself three times before Summer fully understood him.

Got to run, she said to Winter. *We can chat later, if you want.*

Can't you skip? He sounded defeated. *I mean, it's not like we all go for first-days all the time.*

No! Her blaze shot sky-high, making Autumn leap a good three miles backward in shock. *Season-changes are special! Besides, it's* Spring *before me. I want to make sure my time will be remembered. She's gotten slack this year; not as many flowers as last. I have to outdo her, don't you see? This is important!* Still furiously flaming, Summer departed at a run, leaving a burning trail behind her.

Goodbye to you too, snorted Winter. Autumn, having returned, joined him on the step.

What's up with her?

Winter shrugged ruefully. *Oh, you know. Just the usual.*

And what the heck is that supposed to mean? Autumn looked sceptical.

It means whatever you want it to mean. Now, rather than sit out here waiting for everything and nothing, don't you think we should go inside?

Autumn shook his head. *I can't stay.*

True, Winter mused. *But you can visit. Spring's probably back by now; I know she'll be particularly glad to see you.*

Autumn shrugged. *I guess I* could *use a break from travelling.*

Together, they stood up and entered the house.

Dreams.

Our revels now are ended. These our actors,
As I foretold you, were all spirits and
Are melted into air, into thin air:
And, like the baseless fabric of this vision,
The cloud-capp'd towers, the gorgeous palaces,
The solemn temples, the great globe itself,
Yea, all which it inherit, shall dissolve
And, like this insubstantial pageant faded,
Leave not a rack behind. We are such stuff
As dreams are made on, and our little life
Is rounded with a sleep.

-Prospero, The Tempest, Act IV, Scene I by William Shakespeare

Memento Mori by Kailen H.

The first attack was a surprise although it shouldn't have been. We were celebrating a minor win, with beer bottles in our hands instead of our weapons. It was arrogant of us to be honest; we assumed they would be mourning their losses so we never saw the retaliation coming. Our guards were down and the enemy seized the opportunity to swoop down from above to drop Five-Nines on us.

It takes a couple of hits before we are struck out of our drunken stupor and pushed into action. Blood splashes across my face and I can't stop myself from sending a little prayer to God that I survive this. There is a scramble for our semi-automatics and our assault rifles, while some are diving for cover dragging the wounded to safety. Behind me someone is shouting out a warning but he's cut off halfway by the bullet to the back of his head. John's eyes are still open even in death. This boy—no, man—was my best friend for as long as I can remember and all he is now is another lifeless body. Red haze clouds my vision, the Beretta is in my hand and I shoot the scumbag that shot him without blinking an eye.

He's dead before he hits the ground.

In a war, there is no winning. You might *gain* something, but you also *lose* something. Everyone—soldiers and normal folk—loses something in war. There are no 'winning' battles, only struggles to be fought. For every conquered situation, a plethora of lives are lost and all that's left is a sea of broken hearts and spirits. Blood taints your hands and it is blood that taunts you, haunts you in your nightmares.

In the fight for your country, families lose their loved ones when they are welcomed into Death's cold embrace. It is a

Memento Mori

duel to the last living second and when it's over there are only those who have seen too much and pushed too far. The bodies coming out from the war will be just that—bodies, for their souls have been broken by the phantasms of guilt and pale faces.

All that's left to do in the aftermath is mourn, rebuild and remember. There is no celebration, no catcalls of triumph or victorious laughter; not from the survivors for when they do start to jeer and cackle at the mangled, bloody bodies at their feet, they have lost their humanity. And when they take joy in painting the sky with murdered red, they would have lost everything.

"Military glory—that attractive rainbow, that rises in showers of blood—that serpent's eye, that charms to destroy..."
—Abraham Lincoln

There is no happily ever after in war. The ending we get is twisted into a wicked dream of empty eyes and demons against a sky smeared in dried blood.

Son, what is this glory they speak of? Is it a feeling, a *moment* of prideful honour? *They* don't know shit about what they're saying. There is no *glory* in killing. You don't feel a profound sense of pleasure when all you can smell is blood, smoke and gunpowder. You don't feel proud when all you can hear is your heart pumping blood into your veins—when every thump tells you that you're still breathing. All other noise is drowned out and nothing stops you from slicing your opponent's throat open when all you can think about is how to stay alive. You think and feel nothing but trained responses when you are fighting for your life. The long hours of combat and tactics training kick in and your movements are dead on. Literally.

No one comes back untainted. What one side does, the other side follows with twice as much motivation. The ruthless chess game is never ending until a player has reached his endgame—his checkmate. Fathers get killed, mothers, brothers, sisters, friends, lovers. You don't get to choose who to kill for if you did, you wouldn't kill any of them. You don't fight for your country, you fight for yourself because you don't want to die and in the heat of the moment, it doesn't register that you just gunned down someone's father. It doesn't occur to you that somewhere, there is a little girl clutching her teddy bear by the door waiting, waiting, for her dad to come home. You don't even think about the woman holding her lover's last letter with white knuckles whilst twisting her wedding band round, and round, wishing, no, *praying* that her husband will reach home safe and somewhat sound. People are killed every day in a war but she can't help but hope that her husband won't be one of them.

And then, your partner-in-combat is gone and the world of survivor's guilt threatens to overwhelm you. You wish and you wish that you had trained harder so that maybe you would have reached him in time even though you know it wouldn't have changed a thing.

When the war is dead and gone, you don't hear the doorbell ringing or see the military officer at your door. You don't hear the dreaded phrase "I'm sorry ma'am, but your husband has been killed in action" and you don't see another fall to her knees with tears making new tracks on her already tear-stained face *or* her daughters confused eyes. You don't hear the girl ask "What's wrong mama? Where is papa?" You don't *hear* the soldier's wife explain to her baby girl that

"Daddy's not coming home, sweetheart" or hear the cries of disbelief because "Daddy promised he would always be around. He *promised*." And you definitely don't *see* his wife of eight years crying herself to sleep in the guestroom because she cannot bear to sleep in the bed she once shared with her *dead* husband. But you see the struggle of emotions and you watch the black parade to the graveyard. There is a single white rose on the sleek polished wood placed there by the grieving widow. It contrasts the dark coffin like a euphemism; a badly placed word of comfort filling the quiet period of mourning.

If you know what happens in a war, you won't boast of it which such zeal, like a child desperate for glory. Time after the war is spent weeping and coming to terms with its repercussions. Because no matter how many times you pay visits to his wife and daughter, the creature, Guilt, rears its head and slithers its way into your nightmares. In a war, remember that you will die. Endgame.

Cupping Water by Irene T.

Dreams were useless.

Dreams were fragile. Dreams were breakable, changeable, killable. She thought that dreams were for people who had too much free time on their hands.

She wasn't always like that. There was a time when she and her young, impressionable peers had dreams. Ambitions. Whenever their teacher asked them what their ambitions were she would stick her hand up in the air and answer with a huge grin like the rest of them. She had wanted to be a doctor, because doctors sounded so professional and it was what many people wanted to be. Her so-called ambition fluctuated with her increasing knowledge and ever-widening perception of the world. After a while, she chose to become a veterinarian because she loved animals; she changed her mind less than twelve moons later when she heard that she'd have to dissect animals in class. She loved animals too much to cut them up, thank you very much. So what if she was squeamish about it?

But all those were nothing but childish dreams, untainted by harsh experiences and sharp memories. That was before everything in her life decided to trip up. Spectacularly. Life taught her many lessons, and not all of them were positive. She'd been told that she should face the obstacles and stand up, but there were just some things that she wasn't willing to let go. She tried to glue the ever-shattering pieces back together, but it was like clutching at straws: it was a futile effort. The sense of normalcy she wanted so badly will never return.

Cupping Water

She ceased dreaming big; somehow, the bigger picture, the distant future didn't matter much when her present, smaller dream seemed so unachievable.

She didn't need her life to be a bed of roses, nor did she want it to be. She would be perfectly happy to have a simple life, complete with basic necessities. The said basic necessities, according to Maslow's Hierarchy of Needs, included social needs. Friendship. *Family.* And therein lay the crux of the problem.

People often talked about broken families like it was a bad thing. Oh, it was horrible, she was sure; it was something she did not want to experience as long as she lived (and there are two chances of that happening, she thinks before rapidly shaking her head to dispel the nightmare). If she shook her head hard enough, if she stopped thinking about it, then it wouldn't happen.

It was wishful thinking, a childish way to deal with things, but she couldn't help it. *If you can't see it, it's not real.* It was a mantra she used to deal with ghosts in her bedroom, and she used it now, against the ghosts of a future she did not want. Whether it actually worked was a different matter altogether. The raised voices, the stilted silence, the taut string of stress – all of them were still here. She couldn't bear it, and she wondered how others had borne it before her.

But you see, when the fiasco finally ends in a thousand little prickly, bloody pieces, all you're left with is a sense of despair and desolation. The bitter battle ceases to feed you hope, and that's a good thing because hope is the cruelest poison of them all. Hope was the bait for the crafty fisherman, and she'd swallowed it hook, line and sinker believing that it'll make things all right again.

She has yet to see the results.

Broken families were bad and sad, but hers was *breaking*, and somehow the process was even worse than the aftermath.

The Weather Shop by Jalen F.

Dedication: This piece was written for all who are astraphobic, and for my little grey jay, that you might confront your fears without really getting caught in a storm, and that you might learn to fly properly in bad weather (my jay—not you). You will find, in time, that both are equally important things in life.

 In the Dreamrealm, there is a queer old Weather Shop run by a queer old man which sells various weathers to the general public; caged, bottled, boxed and packaged for any who will pay the price.

 The Weather Shop is impossibly hard to catch, as it moves as frequently and unexpectedly as the wind. If you are lucky, or if you live where the weather is extremely unique, you might see it more than once in your life. The Dreamrealm, with its infinite lands, has all manner of interesting weathers to be collected; thus, the Shop travels far and wide at a tremendous speed, seldom staying anywhere for more than a couple of hours at a time.

 Which brings us here, to an expanse of sand and dust as far as the eye can see. Trudging across it as calmly as if this is a walk down the street is a girl of about ten or eleven. Then she sees the Shop.

 She breaks into a run at once. Being a massive structure of flimsy-looking wood often found standing in the middle of nowhere (like now), it is as hard to miss when it is in the vicinity as it is to follow it when it is moving. Multiple layers of colour are peeling off the walls, the wood having taken on a submissive grey hue beneath the many attempts to repaint the exterior. There are shingles missing from the roof, and the simple weathervane crowning the Shop appears to have been charred by lightning. Still, it has the stately bearing of one which has seen a great many things over a great many years.

The Shop might leave at any time without warning; she doubles her speed in fear of missing it. Chances like this come once in a lifetime—or, in her case, twice. She will not let this opportunity slip by simply because she was too slow.

As she tops a dune, time-blackened wrought iron letters come into view, the curling script dancing merrily in an arch over the building. MR WEMBLEY'S WEATHER SHOP, it announces proudly to the world. The somewhat shabby double doors are flung wide open, and a wizened little old man is bent over his cane in the doorway. There is, on the whole, a certain welcoming but yet a hint of forbidding aura about it, like the build-up of wind before a sandstorm that brings both slight relief from the desert heat and an ominous sense of forewarning.

Then she half-runs, half-slides down the other side of the rise, and her view of the Shop is blocked by another towering hill of sand.

From afar, she appears to fly across the desert in her eagerness; a tiny speck of a girl whose feet, oddly, do not quite touch the sand. One can tell, at a glance, that there is something different about her, something more *there*, somehow, than others who inhabit the Realm. There are rumours among the folk here that she is a Changeling, a gift from four of the five legendary Dreamists to their fellow Masterworld-dwelling companion, who can travel between worlds as she pleases. Several dismiss this as a fanciful notion, the result of too much wine before supper. Yet there is *something* that distinguishes her; and, when she is seen in the Realm, she is given a wide

The Weather Shop

berth, regardless of the disputes surrounding her mysterious presence.

But Jalen—for that is her name—wishes to tell her own story, to which she has full rights. And so we return to the desert, where she is swooping down the last sandy slope and waving madly to the old man, receiving a grin and a casual salute in return as she skids to a halt at the door.

"Mister Wembley! Fancy bumping into you here! How's it going with the old girl these days?" 'The old girl', a term only a select group of customers uses, refers directly to the Shop, as they deem the Shop worthy to be considered a person of its own.

Mr Wembley appears quite flustered at this sudden enthusiastic greeting. "Why, if it isn't little Jalen! We're quite well, my dear, quite well indeed. And yourself?"

"The same, thanks for asking. Have you any good new weathers, Mister Wembley? It's been three years—it was right here in the Skrrau Desert that we last met, wasn't it?—and here we both are again! But why? There are so many more places to go! And the Skrrau's weathers are mostly Classics, aren't they? You have plenty of those. Speaking of Classics, has that pesky old Classic Hurricane broken out of its bottle yet? You said it might, three years ago. Oh, I have so many questions for you!" Jalen, who seldom speaks more than two words a year to most folk, is unnaturally talkative around those she knows well and loves.

Mr Wembley laughs. "I suppose I could try to answer some of them. But you'd better step inside and join me for some whirlwind-in-a-cup, as the old girl and I are taking off for the Belving Mountains in precisely three minutes and fifty-two seconds. The Skrrau is merely a brief breather, you see. I'm getting on in years—get a little airsick on long trips these days. I take it you don't mind going off your course?" he adds as an afterthought.

Jalen laughs. "Mister Wembley, you know as well as I do that I never have a course except to follow the Realm where it takes me. And if this isn't taking me somewhere, I don't know what is!" As his smile falters, she realises, too late, that she should not have answered thus.

He gives her an unreadable look before quickly turning to enter the Shop. "Ah, yes. I must've forgotten. Old age and all that. Shall we, my dear?" He gestures towards the dark interior of the Shop. Left unsaid between them as she steps inside is Jalen's reputation for oddness by the Realm's standards, which stretches into a slightly awkward silence as he shuts both doors. Thankfully, the aggressive *Avoid At All Costs!* weathers in the huge floor-to-ceiling displays along all four walls of the Shop are, as always, extremely noisy even through the supposedly soundproof glass, filling the emptiness between the two humans.

Inside, the shop seems even bigger than it looks from the outside, due to the splendid vaulted ceiling that seems dizzyingly far away and the towering heights of the larger weathers themselves. No illumination is required indoors, not even on the darkest of nights, for the blinding flashes of lightning and the soft glow of sunshine, moonshine and starshine in their various containers are an ever-present source of light. There are, however, several floor-to-ceiling windows, interspersed between displays that assist in cheering the place up when the more temperamental weathers are being moody. What little wall is visible is, like the exterior, a weathered grey. Whatever paint once adorned it has been completely worn away. Overall, the room looks tired and resigned, with a hint of fondness for the many weathers it has housed and the one who captures them.

As they move towards the middle of the vast (though largely space-consumed floor-wise by the many weathers for sale) room, the containers on either side decreases in size, the smallest being in the very heart of the Shop. The noise fades away to a soft whisper here, coming from the tiny containers. An elegant spiral staircase winds its way upward, leading the way right through the ceiling to Mr Wembley's private quarters on the second floor. Jalen, forced to drop behind him due to the slender width of the stairs, smiles at the sight of the complete disarray of his rooms, in stark contrast to the neat files of weather classifications and the orderly arrangement of the weathers according to danger scale downstairs.

"Are the whirlwinds still in the bottom cupboard, Mister Wembley?" she asks as they entered the kitchen. Mr Wembley has discovered, quite by accident, that small whirlwinds dropped into cups of tea makes a most excellent, if a little wild, refreshment. As a result, he keeps the tiniest of the whirlwinds he captures for himself and a very select group of customers who appreciate this unique beverage. He has, over the years, taken to keeping them in his kitchen.

"Yes, yes; I'll get the tea," he replies as he scurries over to an angrily whistling kettle and grabs two large mugs. Jalen picks two of the finest whirlwinds from the jars in the cupboard, and, in no time at all, they are chatting away merrily over their whirlwind-in-a-cups. Most of their conversation consists of matters which you would not understand, not having been properly introduced to the Dreamrealm and its ways, and I am afraid I am running out of time and space to tell you. All I can say is that it consists partly of a box, an umbrella, a pine tree and a very wet parakeet, which must not make much sense to you. That's the Realm for you—nonsensical at its best, sensible at its worst, and of course you rather wish to see the Realm at its best. But I am dallying here, which I cannot afford to do any longer. Back to Mr Wembley and Jalen.

Sometime between the making of the tea and the drinking of it, whirlwind and all, the Shop had started to move. Now, it comes to a halt, just as Jalen downs the last of her drink. Mr Wembley looks up at the merry tinkling of a bell hung in the corner of the kitchen, signalling the arrival of a customer. He scurries downstairs, tailed closely by Jalen.

"Wenceslas Wembley, at your service—oh!" Mr Wembley clearly knows the tall, darkly tanned woman whose grim face breaks into a brilliant white grin as she pulls Mr Wembley in for a hug. "Marguerite!"

"And who is our young friend?" the woman, Marguerite, asks, turning her grin to Jalen. *Her eyes are like comets,* Jalen thinks as she reaches out to shake the calloused brown hand Marguerite offers.

"Jalen Fletcher, at your service as well, if I may be of any," she supplies, imitating Mr Wembley's tone.

Marguerite laughs, a rich, fruity sound. "Marguerite Rash. You might have heard of my younger sister, Missy... No? Never mind then. Pleasure to meet you at last, little Miss Fletcher." She shoots an amused look at Mr Wembley before turning back to Jalen.

The Weather Shop

"I believe she prefers Jalen to Miss Fletcher, Marge," Mr Wembly interjects. "Jalen, why don't you do the talking for me here? Refresh your memory of the old weathers and acquaint yourself with the newer ones, eh?" He winks at her. "I'll be getting us all a fresh cup of whirlwind-in-a-cup and perhaps, if you ask nicely, I'll take you both weather-catching in the higher reaches of the Belvings. That's what we're here for, after all. Right, then, have fun!" He promptly scuttles off, leaving Jalen with Marguerite, who continues to smile.

"Are you looking for any weather in particular?" Jalen asks as she begins to show Marguerite around the Shop.

The older woman shrugs. "Just browsing."

"Well, if that's the case," Jalen leads her over to the pride and glory of the shop: the Classics section, "These are the Classic Weathers..."

The afternoon passes gaily. Marguerite is wonderful company, and Jalen takes pride and pleasure in showing off Mr Wembley's seemingly endless collection. From the most modest, most obscure breezy summer's day to the boldest, flashiest hailstorm, the Shop houses them all. There are also many weathers that the Masterworld, where you and I live, does not have, such as belvs and frompi from the Belving Mountains (both of which, by the way, Mr Wembley has run a little short of, which explains this trip to the Belvings) and khrrae and ghadks from the Skrrau Desert. It really is a wonder to see a stormy night in one glass display case and a sunny day in the next, with a very angry tornado trying to escape by hurling itself repeatedly at the glass nearby.

But all good things must come to an end, and the end, for Jalen, comes in the form of Mr Wembley.

"Jalen?" he calls out as he descended the spiral staircase. A huge golden eagle flies alongside, trying not to bump into the glass containers. "This messenger is for you, yes?"

She looks up, sighing. "Yes. Mr Wembley, meet Scythe. Scythe, meet Mr Wembley." Marguerite looks from one to the other, curious, as Jalen strides briskly over to catch hold of Scythe. "I have to go, I'm afraid. It's been so wonderful here with both of you..." She trails off, upset at the thought of not being able to visit Mr Wembley and his Weather Shop again. It is rare enough that she's managed to catch the Shop twice; a third time was unheard of in the Realm. But a summons is a summons, and Jalen knows she can't tarry, lest the portal closes before she passes through.

Mr Wembley seems to read her mind. "I've taught you, of course, the basic methods of weather-catching," he says slowly, almost as if to himself. "Not so very long ago, I discovered that a similar technique can be used to capture sensations." He draws a bottle seemingly out of nowhere, the contents of which were a mass of colours shifting at varying speeds within the glass. "This I made to preserve to memory of the Shop, should anything happen to us both. But it appears that fate has chosen to make this yours." With a flourish, he presents the bottle to Jalen, who accepts it in stunned silence.

"You're sure?" she asks, when she's regained her voice. Mr Wembley holds all his weathers dear, loathing to part with any of them. This, surely, is no different.

But he nods unhesitatingly. "Go," he tells her softly. "Your own world awaits."

She hesitates, smiling ruefully. "This world was mine, too, once. I am a child of the Realm."

"It's true, then?" Marguerite cuts in. "The stories?"

"Most of them," Jalen nods. "Farewell, Mister Wenceslas Wembley, and Miss Marguerite Rash. May we meet again, but if we do not..." She holds up the bottle.

So saying, she runs to a nearby window and, with Scythe at her heels, leaps out.

Libre Enfin, Free at Last by Kailen H.

Dedication: This piece is dedicated to the daydreamers that live to look out windows. You never know what a daydream will inspire you to do. And I hope that one day, your daydreams turn into reality.

Shhhhhhh
The steady sound of rain fills the classroom.
Plip- plop-plip
Trrup- trrup
Bloop- oip- oip- bloop
Plop-plop-plop-plip-plip
Plop-oip-oip-oip

    Raindrops pitter-patter across the roof like the soulful strumming of a guitar; enriching, fulfilling. Tendrils of water weep down the windows, forming puddles when they reach the window sill. In class, a steady dripping of rain falls from the hole in the ceiling and into the red plastic bucket poised to catch it. For a brief moment, I am transfixed on the water's motion. Ceiling. Bucket. Ceiling. Bucket.

    A gust of wind blows the window open and carries me high into the sky. Up there, I am a bird with powerful wings, free to fly amongst the clouds as part of the storm. Endless power rolls across my wings, embedding, manifesting itself in my soul to release massive bouts of thunder and lightning. The howling winds carry me over the white-capped mountains of Switzerland and down again to just touch the oceans.

    I am back in human form now on the back of Buckbeak the Hippogriff, arms wide open, big smiles and shouting as loud as I can. When I lean forward to touch the sea, I feel his soft feathers brushing against my face and I laugh in delight.

Libre Enfin; Free at Last

A tail flicks out of the vast waters and splashes water at me, causing Beaky to buck and swoop into an upwards climb, unfortunately dropping me in the process. I'm falling and falling into the mouth of the hungry ocean below, slowing and slowing as if I had the magical flying umbrella from Mary Poppins before being graciously dropped into the warm Caribbean waters by the arms of the sky.

So down, down I go, deeper into the depths of the crystal clear waters, watching as dolphins and turtles swim by me. It really is a different world under the sea. A sense of panic overwhelms me when I realize that I cannot breathe underwater and a couple of breaths escape me. I watch as bubbles float out of my mouth in amazement, rising and rising higher towards the surface. When I look down, I see a mermaid's tail instead of my own two feet. And it is that tail that propels me forwards and upwards to swim alongside the dolphins, friends as close as kin to my kind.

Playful and sweet and kind, joy is an emotion already born in a dolphin; one that is always growing due to their playful nature. I let out a small giggle as bubbles stream towards the sun and, this time, I follow it upwards with a strong swish of my tail, bursting out of the waters and back into the awaiting folds of the sky.

Snow white feathered wings grow from my back, light but perfectly capable enough to fly me up into the clouds, close to the heavens. I land softly on a cloud and lay on my back staring at the higher puffs of quite solid water vapour, looking for shapes. A dog and its owner come to life; the dog walking its human to make sure the boy is exercised and healthy. Bees gather pollen from a bush of flowers to make their delicious satin-smooth honey, and further to the left, a bear tries to knock down a beehive for the sweet and sticky liquid.

I let the gentle wind sweep the cloud as I look down on the world below; from the bustling city streets of New York. Oh look, a flash mob! Then, off I go to watch gladiators fight at the Coliseum in Ancient Rome. From there, I am swept to the rolling green hills of Australia to run with the wild Brumbies and, finally between the valleys of Scotland to visit an ancient castle.

Church bells ring from the towers of the ruined century-old castle and I jump off the cloud and follow the path leading up to the crumbling palace. Colours swirl around me the moment I enter the castle as dirt and ash blow past me. An echo of an orchestra plays its tune and I find myself in the ballroom with ghosts of people dancing around me, their sashes twirling in an array of silks, satins and chiffons, their laughter surrounding me. Glasses clink together in symphony as a glorious tribute to celebrate life and love. The sounds sink into me, the colours overwhelm me, and I find myself laughing along with the ghosts of the past.

A warm breeze blows, gently caressing my face and in my mind's eye I catch a glimpse of the Brazilian rainforest topped generously with green. Within a second, I find myself flying once more as a bird above the trees and mountains of Brazil. I break out into giggles as I fly alongside a toucan, inhaling the sweet mountain air and –

"Sarah, pay attention!" I was thrown out of Brazil and back into the harsh reality of school, and my teacher who is glaring at me from the front of the class.

"Sorry teacher" I replied, my face heating up slightly at being caught. I'll just have to be more careful next time.

"How do you expect to learn anything with your incessant daydreaming?" she harrumphed and turned back to the board. "As I was saying ..."

I started to tune her out again and took one more longing glance at the open window. The sky was still crying, and I could already feel myself drifting away, itching to reach up to console it. I shake myself lightly to bring myself back to school and tear myself away from the window. With a sigh, I begin to focus on the lesson on the board.

The alluring call of my dreams will just have to wait until I reach home.

Tidbits.

Bits and pieces flung into the universe, sticking in the sky like cotton balls on a jet black velcro surface.

-Bradley Chicho

Rain, Rain, (Don't) Go Away by Irene T.

Dedication: To my fellow crazy writers, continue spinning madness—it makes the world go round. Cheers!

Everyone likes different things. She likes rain. Her heart thrills whenever she glimpses sluggish fat clouds in the darkening sky. It is like that now. Soon it will fall; she can see it in the blood-red glares of a black evening. She smiles. Tonight will be a wonderful night.

For now, she turns to the luminous screen of her sleek silver laptop. Her hand cups the wireless mouse; in two deft clicks she has music flowing from her speakers, plangent and tranquil, occasionally punctured by a distant, approaching thunder. The heralding wind harasses the old mango tree outside her window; its poor branches, already sagging with yellowing fruit, groan pitifully. *It's okay*, she whispers to it. *It's only a storm. It will pass.* The tree drops a ripe mango and falls silent.

The evening clouds over some more, and a light, tentative *pitter-patter* comes into play, a gentle pianissimo. Sometimes the rain doesn't come slowly; it comes in huge torrents, in sudden, gargantuan amounts that make seas seem puny. But it is a gradual one this time. A fairy's touch, she used to call it, when she was younger – back when even the most mundane seemed so very magical. Ah, how bittersweet the memories!

The LCD screen glows brighter in the waning light. Her personal belongings are in disarray around her, stuffed into all the wrong niches. Oh well, that is inconsequential, although her mother will nag. She sighs and types some words into the Google Search engine; the taps, she realizes,

Rain, Rain, (Don't) Go Away

gradually synchronise with the susurrus of water droplets outside. She glances out of the window.

It is dark, although her digital clock blinks only six. Rain dances, shrilly, on the zinc roof above: still a slow *adagio*, but it looks promising. She can smell it in the air – crisp and damp and dewy, all at once. She reverts her attention to the laptop. The search results have loaded – finally! – so she starts sifting through them for her assignment, the troublesome thing.

The increasing cadence of the rain pilfers the next song, but that's okay. She knows it by heart. The drizzle falls heavier now, and faster, almost matching the pace of *tappity-taps* from her keyboard. Everything else is quiet. However, the rain calls to her. *Come*, it seems to say. *Come watch me*.

How wistful it makes her! She remembers how she used to run out whenever it rained and stand in the backyard soaking up God's gift – or are they His tears? She used to wonder about that. She wondered why colour bleached from rainy skies, she wondered---oh, she had wondered about many things, back then.

Her penchant for rain never changed, though. She still laughs when she feels it between her toes and behind her ears, although the rain chills her and blues her lips. Her mother drags her back into the house once she spots her. She always does. Then she is confined to the house, swathed in blankets and a cup of Milo in her hands, but even then she doesn't stop watching the rain.

She can't remember when exactly she has come to be at the windowsill, but she sits there now, with one palm pressed against the biting cold of the glass pane. Her assignment lies abandoned – she wonders if she should save it, but she does nothing. The rain peppers the windowpane: *"Come, come, come,"* it says. How lovely.

Soft music continues to permeate the room, enhancing the ambiance of the sole golden-red flame that lights her room. It reminds her of those luxurious restaurants back in Kuala Lumpur. She knows well the longing that gnaws at her – and at her empty wallet. Such is the life of a kampong girl.

The rain outside has developed into a full-blown storm. Sheets and sheets of vicious needles lash against her window, smacking her palms numb. Truly it is a marvellous show. She loves its freezing rage; its roaring gales that weep, seemingly, for the miseries of the world, drowning its sins.

Its volume is now a fortissimo, loud enough to quell her music. She does not care, not even when, in a flash of impressive lightning, her laptop and its bleating song whites out. Distractedly, she wonders if she should be furious. If so, whom at? The rain? How ridiculous.

It has been some time since she has enjoyed the rain like this. In Kuala Lumpur they were elusive, invisible beyond windowless, claustrophobic walls. In the rare times that she did go out in the rain, her worn Wellington boots scudded concrete and longed for the rich soil of her homeland. It just doesn't feel the same.

She watches the mourning sky with a smile, not even flinching when white-hot lightning slashes the night into half. The sound of rain pounds in her ears and on the glass pane that separates her from it. She can hear her mother calling in

Rain, Rain, (Don't) Go Away

the distance; she yells a reply but stays by the window, still entranced.

The storm rages well into the next hour: seven o'clock, eight o'clock, nine o'clock, and it shows no sign of abating. The countryside is turning into a sea of mud, glistening like slippery skin whenever lightning flashed. She witnesses all this from behind her window, snug and safe and happy.

The tempest reminds her of her temperamental little brother, of his violent reactions and brash decisions; her little brother who is no longer *little* and who now mans the paddy fields with her father. They will have been caught in the storm, she realises, euphoria momentarily forgotten. Or did they get home on time?

A quick check outside assuages her fear: their bicycles are already parked beside the front door, and slick boots are lined, upside-down, against the wall. She can see her mango tree whipping about. The call of rain is much louder here. She hesitates, then crouches at the doorstep to watch the rain. Her bare toes soon get caught in the wet crossfire of a storm.

Rain, she muses, is beautiful in its simplicity. It throws tantrums when angry and frolics when in play – it wears its heart on its sleeve, if it has one. There is no hiding. It takes life, and it gives life, with neither compunction nor cruelty. It is what it is: rain.

The climax begins to simmer down. The darkening sky stops belching angry tears. Its sound dwindles. Sulkily it showers a few final hiccups, then it subsides, wrath temporarily appeased. By half past ten only fat, lazy drops remain, dripping at leisure from leaves and zinc.

She retreats back indoors, opens her diary, and starts to write.

Dear diary, her pen scrawls, *there was a storm today. It lasted a while. It killed my laptop (and my assignment!), so I'll have to work off its repair fee before the semester starts. Jeez.*
I haven't seen a storm like this in ages! KL has nothing like it. Somehow even storms are unique to places, eh, diary? I'm glad I can see it rain here before I go back again.

She pauses to look out of the window.

But, you know...the best things in life?

They aren't things.

Pen and Pencil by Kristal L.

Dedication: This story is for those for whom it was written.

You know who you are.

001.
It is at times like this that he wishes he had more ink.

002.
She's copying 'Ode to a Lizard' by Pablo Neruda. Her words are swift and small, spilling clearly (if not neatly) across the paper. He wonders how such a small slip of a thing could write as beautifully as she does.

"Hey," he says, in passing.

She is too engrossed in her work to notice, let alone reply.

003.
Sometimes, he thinks that she is dancing as she moves.

004.
(She's so tired; she can't quite stand upright, and lying down only increases the ache. She is worn down and used, a mere stub of the fresh, youthful image she once presented.

The sudden drop knocks the wind out of her, and everything goes mercifully black.)

005.
He looks out for her in school today. Oddly enough, she is nowhere to be found, not even when the bell rings for the start of classes.

He frowns.

Oh well; maybe she'll show up tomorrow.

009.
Five days. It's been five days. He hasn't seen head or tail of her all week.

He's very worried.

017.
She's losing track of time.

She doesn't mind not being in class as much as she does the deep, pervading sense of loneliness and abandonment that echoes through her soul. Every moment is a living nightmare of *Where am I?*

When will they come for me?

*Will anyone **ever** come for me?*

022.
Seventeen days.

Life has lost its meaning for him.

023.
(Why?)

032.
He finds her when he gets lost.

(But, they are both lost until they are found once more.)

057.
"So… remind me again, what else is there to do here?" he asks, sarcasm dripping from his voice like melted wax. She rolls her eyes at him, then smiles.

She doesn't really talk anymore. He wonders why.

063.
A toddler stops right next to them on its way to somewhere further than here. It notices her and giggles, shy with the exhilaration of discovery. She, with her abundant creativity, sketches a crude stick figure and a house for it. The toddler, delighted, runs off with the drawing, leaving her behind.

This hurts. *She* hurts. He can see the agony of abandonment reverberate in her eyes.

Me, he wants (but doesn't dare) to say. *There's me. I won't leave you behind, ever.*

She is inconsolable. He cries for her, silent cobalt tears glimmering in the dying evening light.

110.
It's been so long, so very long since she, then he, came to this place of no return. The bitterness of neglect possesses them both.

201.
He bleeds for her out of desperation, a need to make her happy once more. A little blue daisy pools neatly on the grass as she watches him.

She smiles, if only for the briefest of moments.

He is complete.

364.
The sky falls on them today in the shape of some giant's shoe. He is bruised, battered, soiled—but not broken. When the pain recedes, he glances down, aware of a light weight resting gently against his midriff.

She lies partially across him, her body snapped cleanly in half.

365.
Three hours after he bleeds his last, they are discovered by a particularly observant child. The child is sad for them, but it is too late. The pen, and the pencil he loved, are dead where they lie; lost and forgotten nearly a year ago, in the middle of the playground outside the village school.

The Dreamer's Chase by Kailen H.

Dedication: To those who feel as though you're alone, I may not understand all that you go through (really, there is no way I could) but just know that there is always someone out there who is willing to listen. There is someone out there to stand right next to you—someone who will carry you through the storm (or at least, walk through the storm with you).

You are not alone. Hope is so much stronger than fear.

This is for the broken. This is for the ones who feel as if the world is against them, those fighting battles everyday. This is for the wanderers who find no answers, the broken-hearted. This is for the fighters and for the survivors. This is for humanity.

I found her on the swing in the playground, her eyes staring into the prussian-cobalt blue sky. The moon was shining down on her, a pale luminous light on her face. Slowly, I snuck behind her and poked her side. When she turned to me, I made sure she could see my lips clearly before I said "Found you!" I grinned widely. "Were you hiding here the whole time?"

"To be fair, I wasn't hiding", she spoke and signed, her hand movements smooth and precise from years of practice. Laughing, she continued, "I didn't even have to try, you just ran off to 'look' for me. You didn't turn around once to check."

A long time ago, people often asked me, "What do you want to be when you grow up?" Back then, times were simpler and ambitions changed overnight. Nowadays, I find myself saying "happy" more often than not. "When I grow up, I want to be happy. I want to be happy with my life; I want to be happy with myself." I didn't want to be anything else but happy.

You could call it a phase or a point of time or even a moment in time, but everyone goes through a period in which they 'search' for themselves. There is a time when everything passes by in a blur and you find yourself drowning in a sea of moments and memories you want to keep. Everything is filled with so much sadness that all you can do is stare at a spot on the wall and over think. That part of my life was grey and dull like unpolished gunmetal. Voices constantly criticized me, judged me—they weighed my worth and found me unworthy. The world was watching me, waiting for me to fall; waiting, waiting, just waiting for me to shatter.

No one understood what it *felt* like—or, at least, that's what I thought. Most didn't care; they were just obnoxiously curious. Sleeping was hard and waking up was even harder. I was alone in a world of darkness. Most days, I would lose the ability to speak, let alone live my life to fullest. No matter how deep I buried my problems, they would come right back to eat at me from the inside out.

I lost myself in my whirlpool of self-pity, self-hate and soul-eating emotions. I lost my purpose in life and I didn't know who I was anymore. I was paranoid and self conscious; I kept looking over my shoulder just waiting for the other shoe to drop. After all, Fate had already made me deaf, so there **must** be something else just waiting to cripple me further.

The Dreamer's Chase

When I looked into the mirror, I didn't know the girl looking back at me. She looked so sad and so lonely—oh so very lonely—in a monster-filled world she built for herself.

Nothing made sense, so I ran.

I chased after the wind, chasing after it to look for answers without questions. I was on a quest for the truth. I ran for the journey of discovering myself, fuck the consequences. I wanted out of my world of nightmares. I wanted rest and peace in my mind. I wanted to fix my heart that had broken in the battle with my mind. The battle might have been lost, but the war was not yet over. It was far from over.

She was on the swing again. She was laughing at nothing; maybe she was reliving our memories as kids. Seeing my shoes, she looked up at me.

You weren't in school today, I signed in slow, lazy strokes.

She stared darkly at me before replying, *I didn't want to watch people tell me I'm useless. I didn't want to walk around school knowing that they're saying horrible things that I can't **hear**. I didn't want to walk around school **knowing** that they're talking about me behind my back. They've resorted to that now—talking behind my back—because they realized I could read lips. Cowards, all of them.*

My replying strokes are faster, more precise. *You know you shouldn't be paying attention to them. They're wrong about you. Everything they say is a lie out of jealousy.*

"Oh, George," she said, her words stilted and her voice hoarse from lack of use. "They have nothing to be jealous about. At least they know who they are. The things they say are only a more cruel version of the truth. Me? I'm still looking for me. The truth, blunt and simple."

The thing is, the journey is different for everyone. And it is lonelier than anyone could imagine. I need to say this because I know that there are people out there who say all these things don't happen. But they do. I know they do, and I want you to know that you're not alone. There are others next to you. The world isn't as dark as you think.

It took me turning seventeen to finally realize that I still have my whole life ahead of me. I am *not* destined to spend my life as an old spinster, and the world isn't painted in monochrome. Instead, it is swirling with the light. The only thing keeping me in my dreary dimension was myself. The only things eating my insides were teeth my mind created.

And then, there are some people who forget what it's like to be sixteen when they turn seventeen. Everyone is in such a rush to grow up, to throw away their youth. But I know better. I know these moments will become bedtime stories one day, and our pictures worn out photographs. But right now, these moments aren't stories.

They're happening.

You are precious. You are beautiful. You are magnificent. You are loved. Most importantly, you are alive. Never, ever give up hope. Keep fighting, keep pushing, keep surviving.

Someone once told me that we should not chase the wind; the wind should chase us. So when you do catch hold of it, take a good hard look into it—find yourself—and wake up into a world of colour. See life pulsing with, well, life. Feel the wind whirling around you and, when you're ready, let it go. Let it go and ***run***.

I find her on the swing. She's always on the swing. This time, though, she isn't staring into the abyss, nor is she laughing into air. No; ***this*** time, she is giving me a toothy grin, one I haven't seen in a long time.

What? I sign. *Am I breaking out into blue spots or something?*

Her tinkling laugh rings out all around me. *No. I've just realized who I am. My name is Eowyn Grace Miller, and I am no one else.*

end.

Closer To Us by Kristal L.

Dedication: For both parents in equal measure. (But the Frankfurter is for my mother.) With love, your daughter.

Sort of a Prologue

The author of this piece is a quiet, incessantly curious girl who loves words to the point of obsession.

She does solemnly swear that she is telling the truth, the whole truth and nothing but the truth, so help her God, when she says that this story is about ninety per cent truth and ten per cent embellishments.

It is told from the point of view of a person very like the author ten years ago. To assist in picturing the thoughts of a four-year-old sesquipedalian, there are several glimpses into her mind situated within the [brackets] located here and there in the story.

Of course, this is not a full or entirely accurate account of what really happened.

But, as she says not very much further down on this page, stories are like that. There are the important bits and the moderately important bits and the unimportant bits. You have to pick which ones you want to put in, like choosing condiments for a hot dog. In the end, it all depends on the author, even if she's not the one who's going to eat the Frankfurter.

She hopes you will enjoy the words she has put together here especially for you.

Closer To Us

It must have been your curiosity that brought up the subject. Perhaps you went about sticking your nose where it didn't belong; perhaps it was she who happened to let it slip in the most matter-of-fact way that you invariably picked up, as children are wont to do. Whatever the case, the topic arose, which is what really matters.

[Stories are like that. There are the important bits and the not-so-important bits and the unimportant bits. You have to pick which ones you want to put in, like choosing condiments for a hot dog. In the end, it all depends on the author, even if she's not the one who's going to eat the Frankfurter.]

You asked her if she had cancer.

She said that yes, she did, but it was a long time before you came into existence and you shouldn't trouble yourself with it.

Of course, that only piqued your interest. You pressed for more details: does it hurt, can you catch it, how's it made, where'd you get it, what is it?

She took in a deep breath.

It hurt sometimes and didn't other times, you can't catch it, it's made when some crazy cells in your body turn even crazier in a different crazy than before, and she got it from herself (which didn't really make sense, but was an answer nonetheless).

The dictionary answered your last question.

cancer *—noun 1. a malignant and invasive growth or tumour, especially one originating in epithelium, tending to recur after* *excision and to metastasize to other sites. 2. any disease characterized by such growths.*

[Say what?]

She laughed at your bewildered expression and explained, simply, that cancer is a condition in which those crazy cells get out of control and multiply the way cells do to form a huge ugly lump somewhere in your body.

Where?

It depends, she answers. Depends on what type of cancer you have. If it's lung cancer, it's in your lung. If it's foot cancer, it's in your foot. Hers was nose cancer, so it was in her nose.

You ask her what it was like, and she tells you. But that's not really important, so we'll leave that out.

It had been several years before anyone realized she was that sick. She'd sought out the treatment immediately, but hopes weren't too high. There had been no improvement, only a steady decline in health with the end of life's road in sight.

She'd been desperate.

Your parents weren't really a part of any religion then. They'd both been practicing Buddhists during those halcyon days of childhood innocence, but attending mission schools later on saw them to chapel every Monday morning.

It was the latter belief that kicked in as she sat, numb, in the living room of their small apartment. The professionals had given up hope; what more the helpless patient?

But when human hands fail, people turn to the One whose hands will not.
[Whathappenedwhathappenedwhathappened?]

She called out, for the first time in thirty-three years, to a God she'd always thought of as cold and distant.

And guess what?

He answered.

Myriad shafts of light seemed to seep into her frail frame. For a moment, the world was still, bathed in the glory of His love.

When it had passed and she could breathe once more, she was healed—just like that. She just knew, somehow, that the malady that had seized her once would never trouble her a second time.

[Wow.]

She dropped to her knees and sobbed, giving thanks to Him.

That was where her husband, your father, found her when he returned from work, looking better than she'd looked in ages.

She told him what happened.

And he, too, dropped to his knees and sobbed, giving thanks to the One in whose hands every life lies.

Ten years later, you brought up the matter again.

Only, this time, it was for an essay, a story on the day your parents' lives turned a full three hundred and sixty degrees.

[It really should be one hundred and eighty degrees, since three-sixty only brings you back to where you started. But people grow set in their ways and expressions, and you do not wish to go against these unspoken laws of linguistic preservation.]

She tells you again the story of her miraculous recovery—for, in all language's glorious possibilities and time-untouched splendour, there is only that one word that can truly describe His healing power: miraculous.

You write it down, every bit of it, important or not.

Here you are, now, a good fifty years down the road from that day when you were four and blissfully ignorant of your elders' pasts till you asked and she told you.

The two black hearses are marched—side-by-side, as they always were in life—slowly onwards, to be lowered into the earth.

Tears are abundant, family members and friends alike dressed in the dark, sombre hues of the bereaved.

You don't cry. There is only a cold numbness that settles in the place they once occupied (and still do) in your heart.

The sky lightens, the heavy downpour receding for its place in the heavens to be occupied by sunshine.

Closer To Us

You muse, as you watch the clouds drifting unhurriedly across that azure tapestry, that they must be happy now.

As if to reinforce your thought, you think—no, you are absolutely positive that—you see three figures, one with wings and two without, ascend into that glorious sky.
You smile.

Fellow mourners comment that you seem to be bearing this great sorrow with a bold face.

Why cry? He's looking after them now, as He always did while they were here with us. Only, now, He has brought them home, you say.

Several agree that they are much closer to Him and Him to them than when they dwelled upon this earth.

You shake your head. "He is here with us. They're no closer to Him than they were before. It's just that they can see Him now, without fearing His face."

Peace seems to weave a path before you as you depart from their freshly filled graves.

Sort of an Epilogue

Like all good stories, this tale has a moral to it.

It is not long and complicated, nor is it deep and philosophical. It is, however, what I believe to be one hundred per cent true.
It is simply this.

Closer To Us

He is here with us. He is amongst us. He always watches over us, and we are never alone.

He is closer to us than you may think.

Acknowledgements

We would like to thank our parents for feeding us books to read (force fed or otherwise). If that didn't happen, we would have never been inspired to write and bookstores wouldn't have been blessed with all of our allowances, savings, and new year's cash. We would also like to thank Pn. Yow Sow Lay, our former school principal, for supporting us in the project that we oh-so-sneakily kept quiet about until the very end, Miss Loke for her time, and encouragement for this book.

We would like to give special thanks to Ms Tai for proof-reading our book. Enormous gratitude to Miss Yeoh Gim Suan for her advice on book publishing and copyrights, everything would have been mucked up if we didn't have her help.

We would like to thank our English teachers because they push us to thrive, to be better than themselves; as they always say, "be the best, beat the rest!"

We would also like to thank our friends for cheering us on from the sidelines (and their agreement to buy our book). Without them, we might never have gotten the courage to see this book to the end.

And finally, we would like to thank each other because all of us would have gone insane if it were not for the several rant and panic sessions we held.

About the Authors

Aw Siew Bee

Siew Bee is a university student currently based in Kuala Lumpur, Malaysia. She hopes to continue writing even though drowning in assignments is a Very Real Danger. She has yet to decide which one is an occupational hazard: her writing, or her studies? (Hint: University is trying to turn her into a human panda.) She takes up freelancing gigs to cover the crazy living costs in Kuala Lumpur.

Heng Wei Yen

This author is an ordinary girl who likes to test the patience of everyone around her. Though sometimes prone to fickle behaviour (she's trying to fix that, promise), she is in truth, a very awkward girl. She is a major, major Potterhead and **will** threaten bodily harm if you take away her collection. If you value your life you will not even try. She likes to daydream, so don't be surprised if you catch her staring into space.

About the Authors

Shannen Gooi

This author is a perfect example of an angsty teen who indulges in temptations and mistakes. She has had a fair share of mischief and does not intend to stop. Music is her sanctuary, where she seeks refuge, safety and relatability. She loves her family and would like to thank them for their unconditional love and support.

Tan Khye Lin

The youngest of the four, Khye Lin is ironically known for acting like a mother to the others. She likes stationery, clouds and words more than people because you can't use a person to write. (Usually) If needed, she can be found in dark, dusty corners, scrawling absentmindedly in her precious notebook with her beloved fountain pen.

Not all those who wander are lost.

Made in the USA
San Bernardino, CA
26 January 2015